Filumena Press / Fiona Lazar - First Edition
10 9 8 7 6 5 4 3 2 1

Kenzie's Christmas Gift by Fiona Lazar
Illustrated by Angeline Chia

Summary: When Kenzie is reminded that not all kids get gifts for Christmas, she decides to do something special.

ISBN 978-1-946538-00-0

Kenzie's Christmas Gift

Fiona Lazar

Illustrated by Angeline Chia

"It's the night before Christmas," Mama said,
"We're almost ready for Santa in his sled."

Wearing her jammies with Santa stripes,
Kenzie brought cookies of all kinds and types.

Ginger, vanilla, chocolate chip too.
She hid them well, with a single clue.

"Look for me where all the presents shall be,
I'm somewhere near: just kneel down, you'll see."

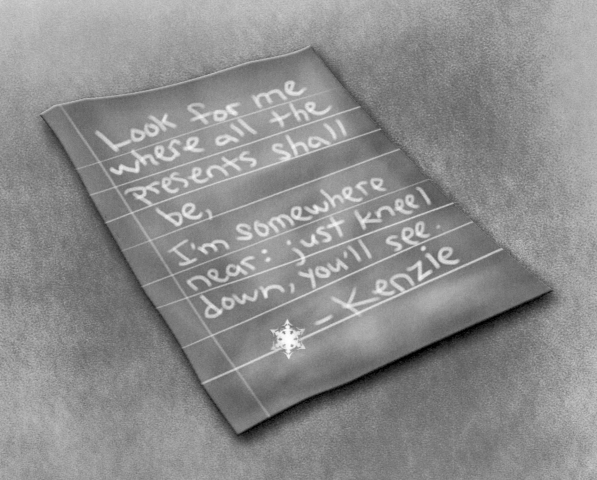

Kenzie giggled as she stashed the sweets.
"I'll catch him this time, once he finds the treats."

Mama said, "Santa Claus comes and goes quick!
He knows his way well down that chimney brick."

"He tiptoes quietly while the children sleep.
And leaves them their present without making a peep."

Replied little Kenzie, "But I won't sleep tonight.
When Santa comes, I'll hold his arm tight."

"First, I'll tell him, that he's my favorite guy!
Then, I'll ask him, how fast does his sleigh really fly?"

"Kenzie, my dear, this is Santa's big night.
Presents he must bring, before the sunlight."

"I know Mama, Santa's a busy guy,
But I must ask him about his sleigh in the sky."

"If I can go up in his sleigh for a ride,
I'll give up my present for a moment to glide."

Mama said, "Kenzie, that's a beautiful thought,
You must be grateful for the gifts that he's brought."

"Giving up presents is a generous deed.
There are kids out there without any toys and many things in need."

Kenzie thought about what her Mama had said.
It's nice to give gifts, joy and love to spread.

Then she remembered Katie, telling her about Christmas day.
"Christmas is about love, not getting presents from Santa in his sleigh."

"This Christmas, Mama, my gift I shall bring,
And leave at the park, underneath the swing."

"My friend Katie, who is scared of the dark,
Every Christmas, with her mom, goes to the park."

"Katie doesn't get toys for Christmas to play.
On the swing, instead, she spends Christmas day."

"On the gift I'll write, 'I'm watching from above.
This is from Santa, To Katie, with love!'"

Made in the USA
San Bernardino, CA
24 January 2017

ISBN 9781946538000

9 781946 538000

MY MONSTER
EATS MY VEGETABLES

WRITTEN BY
KARLIE BURNHAM

ILLUSTRATED BY
ANDREA STEVENSON